SATO
THE RABBIT
A SEA OF TEA

YUKI AINOYA
TRANSLATED FROM JAPANESE
BY MICHAEL BLASKOWSKY

Enchanted Lion Books
NEW YORK

Sato the Rabbit pours a cup of tea.

One day, it becomes a windswept forest.

Another day,
his coffee is a night sky
filled with stars.

What will Sato's drink
become today?

Sato is really looking
forward to teatime. 🐰

WILD RASPBERRIES

Sato the Rabbit sets out
for a forest where wild
raspberries grow.

He picks and tastes
berries as he walks.
Avoiding the bitter ones,
he follows a trail of
sweet ones when …

... he finds an enormous raspberry.

It glistens and looks delicious.

Sato tries hard not to bite right in and carefully removes a piece.

The inside of the wild raspberry room is filled with raspberries.

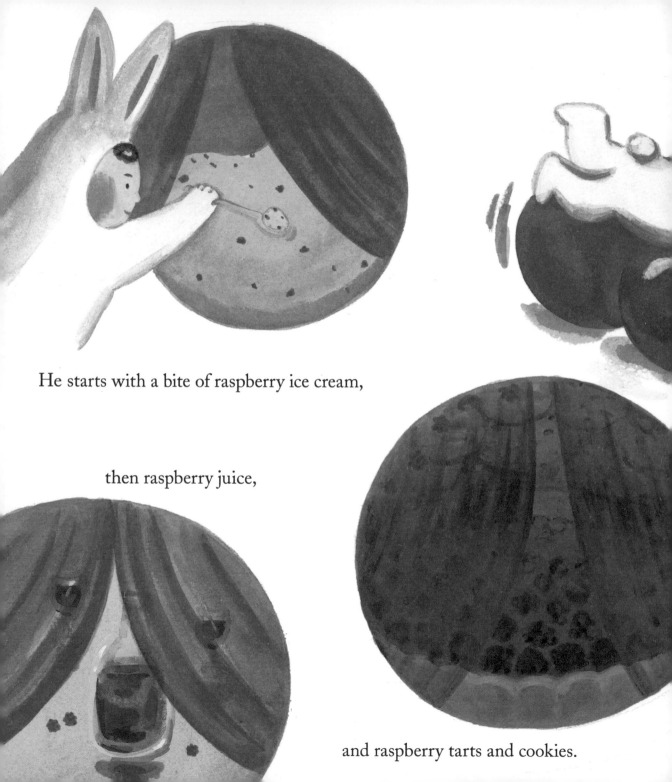

He starts with a bite of raspberry ice cream,

then raspberry juice,

and raspberry tarts and cookies.

Sato rests a while on a wild raspberry cushion.

Next, he eats pancakes bursting with layers of raspberry jam.

When he's completely stuffed, Sato opens a window to get a breath of fresh air.

Even the sunset is raspberry-colored.

BLUE
SKIES

In a clear, bright sky,
a streak from an
airplane appears.

When he sees
another one,
Sato the Rabbit
flies a kite.
The kite has a
fork tied to it.

Sato raises it
quickly, before the
streaks disappear.

The kite rises
higher and higher ...

Frrup

It looks like the fork
has pierced the sky.

Sato slowly lowers the sky to the ground.

He spends the rest of the day
in the sky.

When the sun sets, the stars inside begin to twinkle.

Mistaking the twinkling stars for friends, a group of fireflies gathers around Sato and the sky. ❦

SUMMER
SPOON

One very hot day,
Sato the Rabbit takes out
a small, clear spoon.

He fills a tub with water
and stirs it with the spoon.

The tiny spoon starts
to grow and grow.

Gush gurgle gush

It becomes a waterfall
gushing cold water.

Sato dives
under the water.

When he emerges, the waterfall has become much, much bigger.

The sound of the waterfall is the only thing echoing through the deep, quiet forest.

When night comes,
the waterfall spoon slowly
begins to scoop up stars.

It collects so many.

Sato spends the cool night floating in water swirling with stars. 🐰

A SEA OF TEA

Sato the Rabbit softly stirs
a cup of tea.

He stirs slowly, while gazing
at the evening sun.

A leaf floats in the tea as it
reflects the evening sky.

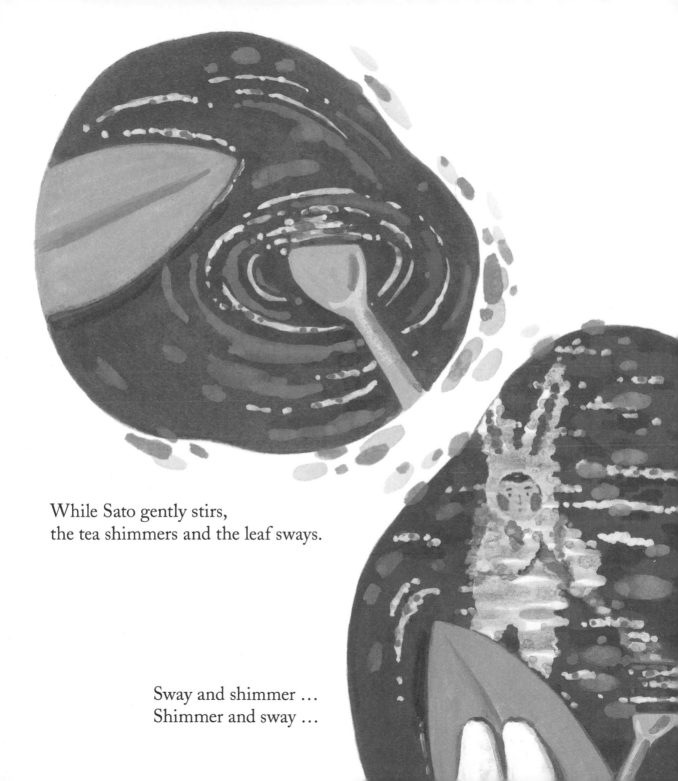

While Sato gently stirs,
the tea shimmers and the leaf sways.

Sway and shimmer ...
Shimmer and sway ...

Sato the Rabbit paddles through a sea of tea.

He pokes the setting sun
with a spoon …

… and scoops up some
of the sun that flows out.

He cuts
a little bit off.

Flip

The moon is almost full.

TUNNEL

Sato the Rabbit is bringing
a cake he baked
to a friend's house.

He takes a shortcut
through a tunnel.

The light inside the tunnel
is a peculiar orange.

Sato and everyone in the
tunnel look different.

The fruits and vegetables are different colors, too.

What kind of painting would someone make inside this tunnel?
Even the color of the golden-brown cake is different.

Sato is a little worried
that the cake might
taste different, too.

It is filled with blueberries.

He takes a little taste
and light leaks out
from the hole.

He peeks inside.

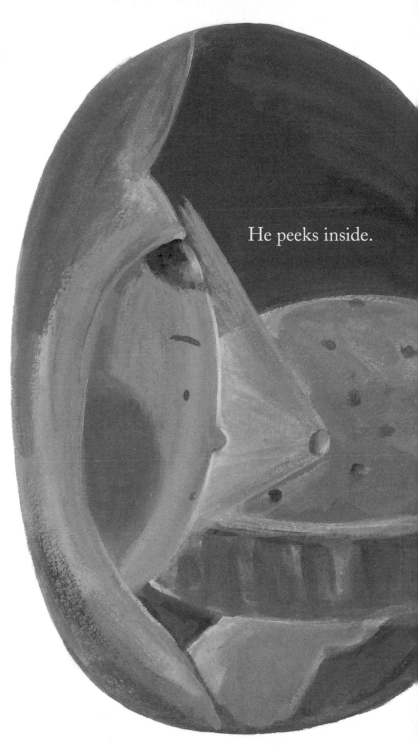

Enveloped in blueberry-colored light,
everyone is enjoying tea and blueberry cake.

Sato hurries to his friend's house so they can eat cake together. 🐰

SNOW
AND STARS

One snowy night,
Sato the Rabbit scoops up
some snow from the top
of a tall tree.

He pours a specially made syrup
onto the crunchy snow …

… and a star floats
down from the sky
while he eats.

The star nibbles the syrupy snow …

... and disappears
into the sky.

The next day,
it looks like it
will snow again,
so Sato fills up
a big jar with
the special
syrup and
goes outside.

From the top of the tallest tree by the forest skating rink, he sprays a snowy cloud with syrup.

When the cloud has soaked up all the syrup …

SKATING
TONIGHT

Sato hangs
up a sign.

Night falls and
it begins to snow.

Stars fall along with the snow,
chasing after the sweet syrup.

Every inch of sky shines
with starlight.

As the stars and snow continue to fall, everyone enjoys a leisurely skate until late into the night. 🐰

BLANKET

One morning after all
the snow has melted,
Sato the Rabbit …

... sets his blanket outside in the sun.

Then he spreads it out on top of some dried grass and has a picnic. When he does …

... spring arrives on the blanket.

Next, Sato ties a rope between some dried branches ...

... and makes a tunnel with the blanket.

When he looks through
to the other side of the
tunnel…

... it is spring. 🐰

www.enchantedlion.com

First English-language edition, published in 2022 by Enchanted Lion Books,
248 Creamer Street, Studio 4, Brooklyn, NY 11231

ISBN 978-1-59270-355-5

Printed in Italy by Società Editoriale Grafiche AZ
First Printing